The JOLLEY-ROGERS and the
MONSTER'S GOLD

For Alice
The Pirate Girrrl of Cherrrtsey

First published in the U.K. in 2015 by Templar Publishing
First U.S. edition 2017

Library of Congress Catalog Card Number 2017931930
ISBN 978-0-7636-9292-6

19 20 21 22 23 MNG 10 9 8 7 6 5 4 3 2

Printed in Saline, MI, U.S.A.

This book was typeset in IM FELL
Double Pica and Tree Persimmon.
The illustrations were created digitally.

TEMPLAR BOOKS

an imprint of
Candlewick Press
99 Dover Street
Somerville, Massachusetts 02144

www.candlewick.com

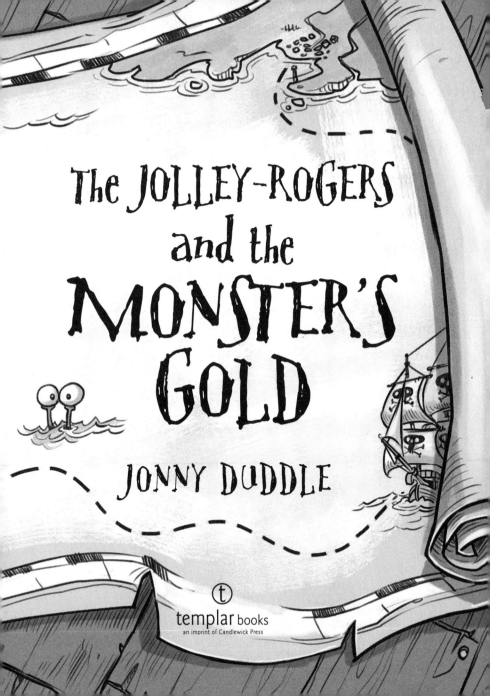

The JOLLEY-ROGERS
and the
MONSTER'S GOLD

JONNY DUDDLE

templar books
an imprint of Candlewick Press

My dear fellow pirate,

Do ye want to be rich?
To get treasure beyond
yer wildest dreams—
to find nuggets of gold as
big as ships' beams?
And diamonds and rubies
the size of yer eyes?
Just follow this map
to claim yer prize!

From,
A friend

1.
BOTTLES

Every Saturday morning, Matilda sat on the dock in Dull-on-Sea harbor and fished for bottles, hoping to receive a message from her best friend, Jim Lad.

Jim was a pirate, and he liked to keep in touch with Matilda by sending notes. When he'd written one, he would pop it into an old bottle, plug it up with a cork, and throw it over the side of his family's pirate ship into the sea.

If Jim had a really urgent message, and they weren't too far from land, he might tie it to the leg of his grandpa's parrot, Squawk, who would fly to Matilda's house and tap on her window. Jim called this "air-mail," but to Matilda it always sounded more like "arrr-mail." But most of the time, Jim's notes arrived in bottles.

Matilda's dad was sitting beside her, fishing for fish rather than bottles. He rarely caught anything, but he had a lot of very expensive equipment and a hat covered with hooks pointing skyward. He'd dozed off and was gently snoring.

Matilda was feeling a bit sleepy too. She was mid-yawn when her fishing line suddenly snagged on something. She sat upright, spinning her reel expectantly, and spotted her hook tugging a faded green bottle across the water. Matilda could see there was a piece of parchment inside! She reeled it in, giddy with excitement, hoping it was a note from Jim Lad.

She wrenched the cork out with her teeth, turned the bottle upside down, and shook furiously. The parchment tumbled out and unfurled to reveal a map.

"Eh? Humph . . . What have you got there?" Matilda's dad mumbled, awoken by the clunk as Matilda put the bottle down. "Another note from Jim Lad?"

3

"Nope! It's a map!" said Matilda, holding the roll of tattered parchment open. "And there's a big red X in the middle, right over a tiny island. Do you think it's a treasure map?"

On the other side of the parchment was a note, but it wasn't in Jim's handwriting.

"My dear fellow pirate . . . Do ye want to be rich?" Matilda read. "Hmmm. Maybe I should write to Jim. He'd be a 'fellow pirate,' and he loves treasure maps. We could go treasure hunting together! And," Matilda pointed out, "Jim and his parents have a ship, which would make searching for a treasure island much easier."

"Good idea," said her dad. "But you'll have to check with your m —"

Before he could finish his sentence, a parrot landed on his head.

"GRUMPY MERMAID!" screeched Squawk. "GRUB AND GROG! TWELVE O'CLOCK!"

"Hooray! Jim Lad's here!" Matilda squealed.

2.
FIDDLE-DE-DEE

"No shark brains . . . ?" asked Jim's dad.

Outside the Grumpy Mermaid Inn, Matilda and her parents were sitting beneath an umbrella, across the table from Jim and the rest of his family. The Jolley-Rogers had arrived in Dull-on-Sea at dawn, and had been stocking up on provisions. Jim's mom had suggested a nice lunch before they set sail again, but Jim's dad was disappointed with the menu.

"Landlubbers eat such boring grub!" he said to the waiter. "Ye'll be tellin' me next ye ain't got no kraken fillets!"

"I'm afraid not, sir," replied the waiter. "All our fish are locally caught. Could I suggest the pan-fried sea bass, with saffron beurre blanc, crushed potatoes, and citrus-infused greens?"

"What'd he say?" asked Nugget.

"Bah, gimme the fish and chips!" grumbled Jim's dad.

"I'll 'ave fish and chips too," said Jim's mom.

"Me too!" said Jim.

"Me three!" said Nugget.

"Fish and chips!" squawked Squawk.

"So, that's four orders of fish and chips, rather than five . . . ?" said the waiter. "I presume your macaw just repeats everything you say. How sweet!" He leaned over to stroke Squawk, but thought better of it when Squawk fixed him with a hard stare, accompanied by a low growl.

"We'll have two fish and chips," said Matilda's mom. "And one sea bass, please."

With the food ordered, everyone turned their attention back to Matilda's map, which was rolled out across the table. Jim's dad also had one of his ancient sea charts and was comparing the two, sliding his compass across the parchment, while muttering to himself and scratching his head.

"Thanks for the map, Matilda. We pirates love a good treasure hunt," he said. "Funny thing is that this 'ere treasure island don't appear on my sea chart. But we could try to find it, all right. . . . I'm partial to a bit of treasure!"

"Me too!" said Nugget.

"Personally, I think treasure causes nothing but trouble!" chirped Squawk.

"Do you want to come with us, Tilly?" said Jim, looking at his mom, who nodded with a smile.

"Yes, please!" begged Matilda, turning to her parents with pleading eyes.

"Oh well, I suppose it would be a nice little adventure for you," Matilda's mom replied. "Do you think it's safe?"

"I'll tell yer true, your Matilda's got a fine pair of sea legs!" said Jim's mom. "The *Blackhole*'s shipshape and the sea's becalmed to Hag's Head and beyond. It ain't much farther to where the treasure is supposed to be, and they ain't talking 'bout rain or storm for a week or more."

"We be needin' Matilda's help," added Jim. "She's got a nose for gold! She found the map too,

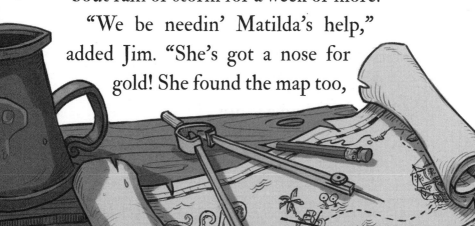

so it'd be all wrong, I'd say, leavin' her ashore!"

"All right, you can go!" agreed Matilda's mom, just as the waiter returned with several precariously balanced plates.

Matilda and Jim dug into their fish and chips, chattering and making plans for their trip, while their parents talked about boring grown-up stuff. Nugget threw her food in the air, one piece at a time, for Squawk to catch. They were just finishing their lunch when they heard the faint sound of a fiddle floating on the wind. The music meandered along the dock toward them.

An old fiddler appeared, and as he fiddled he sang a song:

"I was sailing one day and what did I see?
An island of gold in the scurvy sea!
With a fiddle-de-dee,
there'll be treasure for me.
Fiddle-de-dee, across the sea."

He stopped at
their table, glaring
at the treasure map.
Everyone looked
at the fiddler. The
fiddler looked back
at them. Then he
looked at the map
again. He dragged

his bow across the fiddle strings and burst
back into song.

"As I sailed the seas, I scribbled a map,
so that when I got home, I could
find my way back.
Ye cannot imagine the booty that's there —
a huge haul of treasure
beyond compare!

That map that you have was drawn by me,
adrift upon the scurvy sea.
Perhaps you'd like me to be yer guide?
To find the treasure that I spied?"

Jim's dad clapped his hands together in glee. "Arr! Ye'd be the perfect sound track to our trip. I love a good sea shanty! And I ain't that good at followin' maps, so I'd be most grateful for yer help."

He jumped up and put one arm around the old fiddler. "Back to the ship, me hearties!"

"Tentacle!" said Squawk.

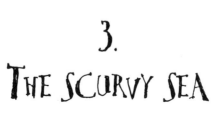

3.
THE SCURVY SEA

It was a short stroll from the Grumpy Mermaid to the Jolley-Rogers' ship, the *Blackhole*. There was a crowd of tourists taking photographs and admiring the ship, which stood out among the gleaming white yachts bobbing in the harbor.

The Jolley-Rogers took up their positions around the deck and aloft, Jim scurrying up the ratlines so that he'd be ready to unfurl the mainsail with his mom. Matilda climbed onto the foredeck with Bones the dog, who propped a paw and a wooden leg on the rail, barking excitedly. On the poop deck, Jim's dad rolled out the treasure map and shouted to Matilda's parents.

"Could ya help us out and unhitch them lines?"

Nugget jumped on her barrel at the helm and, with the push of a big brass button, the *Blackhole*'s engine burbled to life. Matilda's parents each released a rope from a bollard and waved from the dock as the *Blackhole* slipped its moorings and chugged out of the harbor. Matilda blew her parents a kiss, delighted to be heading out to sea on a real treasure hunt.

The fiddler had been playing some rousing shanties, but as they sailed into the open waters of Dullshire Sound, the music took on a more somber tone.

"To find this island, you'll have
to be quick —
for they say it performs a vanishing trick!
And none who've tried to set foot
on its sands
have ever returned to pirate lands."

"What did he say?" mumbled Jim's dad from the stern of the ship, his ears straining to make out the words of the fiddler, who was dancing on the fo'c'sle.

"I ain't sure," said Jim's mom, sliding down a rope onto the poop deck. "But I don't think we shoulda brought him. Ye've a collection of sea shanty CDs, and we could've plugged in some speakers on deck if ye'd wanted a singsong. There be somethin' fishy 'bout that fiddler."

"He said the island does a vanishing trick," said Nugget, whose hearing was better than her parents'. "And the pirates that go there never come back!"

"Well, that ain't right," said Jim's dad, looking through his telescope and admiring the fiddler's balance as he pranced along the bowsprit. "Because he 'imself came back. He's a harmless old minstrel; a salty sea dog with a song to sing. Hard to starboard, please, Nugget! We'll be headin' southeast!"

Through the lens, a gnarly old head came into view, popping up through a hatch on the foredeck. The head was followed by a rusty hook, waved in the direction of the fiddler.

"Uh-oh," said Jim's dad. "Grandpa's awake."

Grandpa turned his face toward the stern, grumbled a few words that were lost on the wind, then disappeared belowdecks with a grimace.

"And he's not happy!"

1.
MONSTERS

Grandpa really wasn't happy.

"I was all cozy in me hammock, havin' an afternoon nap, and I'm awoken by a screechin' fiddle!" Grandpa shouted. "Who is this scupperlout? What's he doin' aboard our ship?"

"Matilda found a treasure map, and it was the old fiddler who scribbled it. Or so he says," said Jim's mom. "My silly husband invited him aboard for the shanties, and hopin' he'd get some help with his map reading."

"Even from 'ere, I don't like the look of him. And brush me barnacles, he sounds even worse than he looks!" said Grandpa.

"He looks a bit like you," said Jim's dad. "But even thinner and less crotchety!"

Grandpa scowled and hobbled across the deck to sit in his rickety rocking chair, pulling the cork out of a bottle of grog with the few teeth he had left. "There are tales I could tell ye, of swivel-tongued scugs who'd show ye their maps and take yer ship to the edge of beyond. I could tell ye of great galleons lost at sea on the promise of a map. Be warned!"

Squawk landed on Grandpa's shoulder, ruffled his feathers, and said, "Tentacle!"

Down at the other end of the ship, Jim had joined Matilda on the fo'c'sle. He was showing her the best way to coil ropes while they listened to the fiddler's latest ditty.

"There is one small thing I forgot today —
There's also a monster, or so they say,
that likes to eat pirates who come
for the treasure,
and chew up their ships,
just for good measure."

"Did ye hear that, Tilly? A monster!" Jim looked worried. "Do ye reckon we should turn back to port?"

"Nah, monsters aren't real," said Matilda. "We learned that in school."

"Yes they are!" said Jim. "I've seen 'em on maps, and I've read 'bout them in Grandpa's old leather books. There's been many a tale of pirates devoured by monsters."

"That's just it, they're tales, told by one sailor to another, and the so-called monsters get bigger and badder each time! There aren't real monsters, only shapes in the water or normal sea creatures . . . whales and sharks and giant squids and stuff. I saw a picture of this really big oarfish once, and it looked like a sea serpent. But it was just a fish, and fish don't eat people, not even pirates!"

Matilda nearly jumped out of her skin when the fiddler's head suddenly appeared over her shoulder, accompanied by the high-pitched screech of his fiddle.

"They ain't just tales! They ain't just whales!
There's a beast out there!
Ye'd better BEWARE!"

And then he was off again, skipping along the bowsprit, with a balance and sprightliness that belied his age, singing about monsters at the top of his voice.

"There's something very odd about him," said Matilda, with her arms folded. Bones growled, his fur prickling along his back.

On the poop deck, Jim's dad was still wrestling with the navigation and hoping the fiddler would give him some help, as he'd promised at the Grumpy Mermaid. "This island don't appear on *any* of my charts, 'tis very strange. Maybe it's just small," he said, "but lookin' at this treasure map, I reckons we'll make landfall before

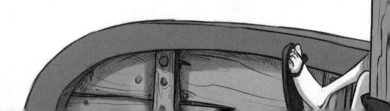

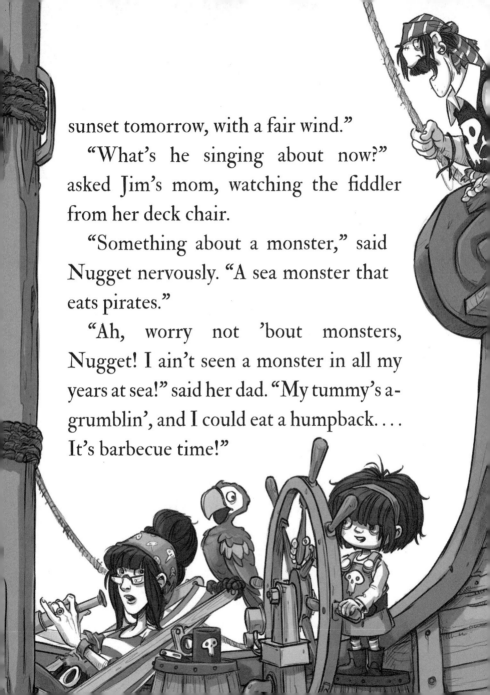

sunset tomorrow, with a fair wind."

"What's he singing about now?" asked Jim's mom, watching the fiddler from her deck chair.

"Something about a monster," said Nugget nervously. "A sea monster that eats pirates."

"Ah, worry not 'bout monsters, Nugget! I ain't seen a monster in all my years at sea!" said her dad. "My tummy's a-grumblin', and I could eat a humpback.... It's barbecue time!"

5.
A Pirate Feast

Mr. Jolley-Rogers had raided the *Blackhole*'s freezer, and a table beside the barbecue was piled high with an array of seafood. He was gurgling grog through two long straws attached to his favorite bicorn hat while frantically flipping food on the grills.

"Maybe ye could sing us a song, old fiddler. Do ye know any shanties 'bout grub?" he asked, popping his head out

of the thick black
barbecue smoke and lifting his goggles.

The fiddler, who had been hunched
over the rail in the corner of the deck,
suddenly perked up and danced
toward them, bursting into song.

"Make no bones about it,
it's a big old beast,
that likes nothing more
than a pirate FEAST.
It can swallow whole ships in its
whirlpool JAWS
(though they say he's allergic
to scarlet macaws)."

"The monster must have a right big mouth," muttered Jim. "Even bigger than Nugget's."

Nugget elbowed Jim in the ribs and scowled, which looked even more frightening than usual because her face was covered in smears of bloodlike ketchup. "Hopefully he'll eat you first!" she said. "And anyways, he might swallow the ship, but Squawk'll be safe, with the monster's allergy 'n' all."

"Tentacle!" squawked Squawk from high up in the rigging.

"Not quite the shanty I had in mind," said Jim's dad, gaping at the fiddler. "Fancy some grub, old man? A walrus kebab? Battered tentacles? Some surf and turf, per'aps? The fish won't keep, and the rat was fresh from the bilges this mornin'!"

"I will be fine! I don't need food!
Unless I be REEEALLY in the mood . . ."

answered the fiddler with a screech of his strings before skipping back to his resting place on the rail.

"He doesn't eat much," whispered Jim's mom.

"That's probably why he's so thin!" said Jim's dad, digging into a barnacle burger. "Sometimes you can hear his bones clacking together as he walks."

"I don't trust him," said Grandpa. "He ain't eaten or drunk nothin' since we've been upon the scurvy sea."

They looked at the fiddler, noticing how his bony limbs stuck out at strange angles and the way his eyes seemed too big for his face.

"He's funny-shaped too," added Grandpa.

"Mom, what's for dessert?" asked Nugget, sucking on the ketchup and fish skin that was stuck to her fingers.

"I think ye've had enough, kids. Ye'll be havin' nightmares if yer bellies are too full, especially with all this talk of monsters. It's time for bed, we've a long day ahead on the morrow."

There were three loud groans.

"But maybe if yer all ready for bed," Jim's mom continued, "Grandpa could tell yer some pirate tales for a little while, just until the sun drops below the ocean."

There were three loud cheers. Jim, Matilda, and Nugget dashed to their cabins to get into their pajamas. But as Grandpa followed them down, a dark and mysterious shadow fell across the deck. . . .

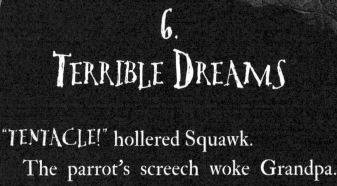

6.
TERRIBLE DREAMS

"TENTACLE!" hollered Squawk.

The parrot's screech woke Grandpa. A moment later, he felt something grab hold of his peg leg. He dragged his eyepatch from his good eye and saw a massive tentacle wrapped around his wooden leg. Grandpa clung on to the edge of his hammock with his hand and his hook as the tentacle pulled him toward the open hatch. He kicked at it furiously with his good leg, while Squawk flew about the cabin, trying to peck at the tentacle. But still it yanked on Grandpa's leg.

Grandpa's cabin door swung open and slammed against the wall as the rest of the Jolley-Rogers came running to his aid. At exactly the same time, with a loud *POP*, the tentacle disappeared through the hatch, taking Grandpa's wooden leg with it into the darkness beyond.

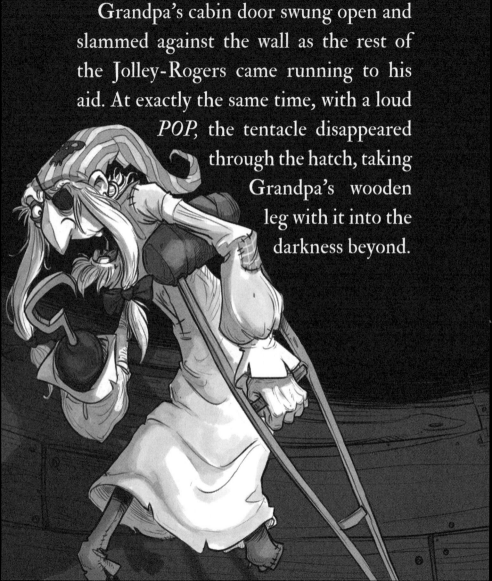

"MY LEG!" shouted Grandpa, leaning out of the hatch. "GIVE ME BACK MY LEG, YE SCURVY BEAST!"

Jim's mom pulled Grandpa back into his cabin. "Better it's just yer leg than the whole of ye," she said.

"Did ye see the beast?" shouted Grandpa, bubbling with rage. "I'll hunt the varmint down! I'll get back me

precious leg! The monster picked the wrong pirate for a fight!"

"We could make you a new leg?" suggested Nugget.

"I don't want a *new* leg!" hollered Grandpa, waving his cutlass above his head. "I want me *old leg*! I've had that peg leg for fifty years! I whittled it from the mast of Black Bob's ship! His cursed cannon took my flesh and bone, so I sank him right there, leavin' just the very top of his mast pokin' above the waves. I took its timber for my peg, figurin' Black Bob wouldn't be needin' it deep down in Davy Jones's locker. It's as good a part o' me as the flesh that were there before.

I'll be gettin' that leg back if it's the last thing I do!"

"Oh. OK," said Nugget quietly.

"Even so, ye'll be needin' a temporary peg, Dad. Just until ye get yer old leg back," said Jim's mom. "We'll figure somethin' out tomorrow."

"You lot, get back to yer bunks," said Jim's dad. "I'll keep watch 'til mornin'."

"I'll take the helm and we'll sail through the night," added Grandpa. "If what the fiddler says is true, we might find that monster guardin' the island. He'll regret he ever crossed old Grandpa Rogers!"

The next morning, Jim awoke to the sound of his dad snoring, just above his cabin.

"He's been doing that forever," said Matilda from the bottom bunk. "It's been keeping me awake since dawn."

Jim opened the hatch above his bed and poked his head out.

"He's never been a good lookout," he said.

His dad was fast asleep in a chair in the middle of the deck, snoring very loudly with a musket across his lap and his headlamp flickering faintly in the morning sun. Behind him, Jim's mom, Nugget, and a particularly grumpy-looking Grandpa were diving into breakfast while being serenaded by the fiddler.

Jim and Matilda climbed out of the hatch and joined them, just in time for another verse, which the fiddler repeated several times.

"There are rubies and diamonds
the size of balloons —
silver and guineas and golden doubloons —
but grab it all quick, or it'll
have your entrails!
Now, fiddle-de-dee, let's trim
those sails."

"Why does he keep saying 'fiddle-de-dee'?" asked Nugget.

"I don't know, Nugget, but all this talk of entrails is putting me off my sausage," said Jim's mom.

"Now," she went on, turning to Grandpa, "what are we going to use for a temporary leg?"

"I can just use me crutch for now," mumbled Grandpa through a mouthful of sausage.

"Nonsense, Dad. Ye can't take on a monster while clutchin' yer crutch. We'll find somethin' and strap yer on a makeshift peg."

"How about this?" suggested Nugget, taking hold of the table leg.

"I think the table needs that one, Nugget," said Mom.

"We could whittle down one of the logs we've got for the woodburner?" said Jim.

"Too short!" grumbled Grandpa.

"There's that old ax handle?" suggested Jim, pointing to a pile of tools leaning against the gratings.

"Too thin!" grumbled Grandpa.

"We don't play the piano much," Jim went on. "That's got thick legs."

"Too fancy!" grumbled Grandpa. "And it's got brass wheels. I don't want wheels."

"How about we go ashore and find a nice piece of wood?" said Matilda. She had been gazing out to sea and had noticed a small shape in the distance, rising from the ocean. "Look, there's an island!"

"Great plan, Tilly! LAND AHOY!" yelled Jim.

"Jim, get yer'self aloft and spread them sails!" ordered Jim's mom. "And Nugget, ye'd better wake yer father, and tell him to find the keys to the car-boat!"

7.
The Island

Jim Lad hopped out of the car-boat with its bow rope coiled around his shoulder. "All ashore, me hearties!"

His dad dropped the anchor while Matilda, Nugget, and Bones splashed through the surf and onto the sand. Jim ran up the beach and tied the rope to a palm tree, to be doubly sure the vehicle wouldn't float away if the tide changed.

"What a lovely spot!" said Jim's dad. "We shoulda brought a picnic!"

"Ye've only just had breakfast," said Jim, frowning.

Mr. Jolley-Rogers took off his flip-flops and climbed out of the vehicle. His tummy rumbled as he paddled through the

water to join the others. He hadn't eaten as many sausages as he normally would, because everyone had been in a rush to find Grandpa a new peg leg. Before he was so rudely awoken, he had been enjoying a lovely dream about a mermaid, but now his memory was getting a bit hazy and he couldn't remember her name.

"Hey ho, then, let's collect a bunch o' timber!" he said, pointing to a wicker basket he'd dropped on the sand. "Move sharply, then we can be gettin' back to the *Blackhole* in time for my mid-mornin' cake!"

"Here's a decent bit of driftwood," said Matilda, picking up a pale, twisted branch on the shoreline.

"Good start, Tilly! Ye can stick it in the basket, but that piece looks gnarlier than Grandpa! I reckon we should be searchin' along yonder tree line for the best stuff." Jim pointed to the dense foliage at the top of the beach.

With all of them rummaging among the undergrowth, the basket soon filled up. But Nugget quickly got bored with collecting wood and wandered along the beach, in search of shells.

"Don't go far!" shouted Jim Lad.

"Aye, aye, Cap'n!" said Nugget, chuckling and saluting as she skipped away.

She hadn't gone far when she met a monkey, sitting on a rock. It was looking directly at her, holding a banana. The monkey popped the banana out of its skin and offered the fruit to Nugget with an outstretched arm.

"Mmm, I am a little hungry . . ." said Nugget, taking the banana and sitting down next to the monkey. But before she had finished eating, the monkey jumped from the rock and disappeared into the trees. Seconds later it reappeared with another banana and offered her that one too.

"Oh, thank ye kindly!" said Nugget. "But one's enough for me. My dad's always hungry. And my brother and his landlubbing friend, Matilda, would probably like a banana. Are there more of them?"

The monkey nodded, chattering wildly as it scurried into the trees.

Nugget shuffled her bottom off the rock and skipped after it.

Farther up the beach, the wicker basket was now full. "One of these timbers must be perfect for Grandpa's makeshift peg!" said Jim's dad. "Back to the boat, urchins!"

"Don't forget Nugget! She ain't returned from her shell collectin' yet," said Jim. "Maybe we should go 'n' fetch her?"

"Aye, but let's jump to it!" said Jim's dad as he placed the basket carefully in the boat, then marched down the beach rubbing his tummy.

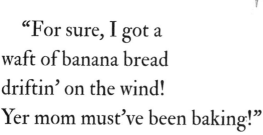

"For sure, I got a waft of banana bread driftin' on the wind! Yer mom must've been baking!"

Jim and Matilda chased after him while Bones ran ahead, weaving across the sandy beach and sniffing. Soon, Bones stopped at a rock and started to bark, snuffling at something. They all caught up with him, only to find Nugget's bag spilling shells onto the ground.

On the rock was an empty banana peel, and beside it were two tiny sets of footprints in the sand. The tracks disappeared off into the trees.

"She ain't alone!" said Jim. "One of them sets of tracks belongs to Nugget, all right. But she's with someone . . . or something. . . . We've gotta find her! Come on, everyone."

Bones had already hurtled into the trees, and Jim followed, drawing his cutlass. Matilda ran after them, leaving Jim's dad alone on the beach, torn between heading back to the ship for some lovely banana bread and searching the jungle for his daughter.

"Curses!" he said. He glanced back toward the *Blackhole*, hoping they'd save him a slice or two, before crashing into the undergrowth.

He caught up with Jim and Matilda in a clearing. Just in front of them, Bones was tiptoeing tentatively toward a pile of bananas on the ground.

"A*rrr*, bananas!" said Jim's dad. "I suppose that's the next best thing to banana bread!"

He took a big stride toward the bananas, arms outstretched. Jim and Matilda tried to grab him.

"DAD, WAIIIII —" shouted Jim.

But it was too late.

The ground shifted, and their feet were whipped into the air. Jim, his dad, Matilda, and Bones tumbled together, squished between the bananas, as they were enveloped in a great net that surged upward. Moments later they were dangling in the canopy, swinging gently between the trees.

8.
MONKEYS!

For a while, nothing happened. Then the smell of squished banana began to attract swarms of flies and bees. Jim quite liked bees, but not when they were crawling all over his banana-covered feet.

Jim's dad was chomping on the last of the un-squished bananas when Matilda spotted a monkey peeking up at her from behind a palm leaf.

Then Jim pointed out two more

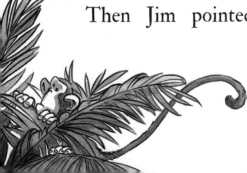

scurrying around on the forest floor, chattering excitedly.

"And there's another!" cried Matilda as a monkey, hanging by its tail, untied one of the vines that held the net aloft. The next moment, the net lurched sideways as the vine fell free. More monkeys then clambered onto the net above them, deftly unpicking the knots.

"I think they're trying to help us!" said Jim.

Matilda watched the monkeys, her eyes following the length of the vines they were untying.

The vines rose upward into the branches and then fell down to

the forest floor, where hordes more monkeys were now running around, whooping and hollering. Some of them seemed to be carrying spears. She spotted another monkey behind a tree, with a tricorn hat on its head. It might have been carrying a funny-shaped stick, but the stick looked a lot like a musket.

"Um . . . I think they're trying to release us, Jim. But I'm not sure they're trying to 'help' us."

"Maybe they've got more bananas!" said Jim's dad.

The net shifted again. Matilda gasped. "It's a long way down. I really hope the ground's soft."

The net swung sideways suddenly and a monkey flew past them, dangling from a vine. More vines whooshed by, and all the monkeys below them disappeared into the undergrowth.

"At least we'll get away from these bees," said Jim.

The next moment, the branch directly above them let out an almighty creak and the net dropped.

THUMP!

They all landed in a heap, still entangled in the remnants of the net. Bones was sitting on Matilda. Matilda was lying on Jim. Jim was lying on his dad.

"It's at times like this I'm glad you have such a big tummy," Jim said to his dad, who was flat out on his back. Mr. Jolley-Rogers groaned a little as his arms flopped out to his sides. Bones growled.

The monkeys were back, murmuring and pointing as they surrounded their captives. Some of the monkeys had spears, and the largest monkey wielded a rusty

musket. On his head was a tricorn hat bedecked with feathers. He barked at the other monkeys in a gruff voice, and they swarmed all over the tangled net.

"Get off me!" screamed Matilda as she was pushed, pulled, and prodded. She resisted as best she could, but lying in a heap beneath the net made it difficult. Vines and ropes encircled her limbs. Monkeys were yabbering and clambering all over their captives in a knot-tying frenzy. Soon Matilda, Jim, and his dad were hanging upside down, strapped by their arms and legs to long poles, and being bundled hastily through the forest. Bones's mouth had been muzzled, and he was tugged along behind them with a monkey on his back.

"I wonder where they're taking us," yelled Jim Lad. "I hope Nugget's there!"

"It's not a big island, Jim," Matilda replied. "We'll find out soon enough."

"Do you think monkeys can bake?" Jim's dad asked.

9.
KING HAIRY TOES

The monkeys and their captives emerged from the forest into another clearing, to the sound of drums, an accordion, and some truly dreadful fiddle playing. There were monkeys everywhere.

"Nugget!" yelled Jim, spotting his sister.

Nugget was at the center of the clearing, sitting on a wooden throne. Her face was covered in paint and she

had flowers threaded through her hair. Beside her was a grizzled old chimpanzee, wearing a crown and dressed in tattered pirate clothes, munching on a banana. On his shoulder was the oldest parrot Jim had ever seen. Most of its feathers were missing, it wore an eyepatch, and its one good eye was closed.

Nugget was drinking from a coconut shell, but when she heard Jim's voice she spat her straw out of her mouth. "Jim!"

"TENTACLE!" hollered the old parrot. Its body stretched tall and its eye almost popped out of its head. It surveyed Jim, his dad, and Matilda, took a deep breath . . . and fell asleep again.

Nugget jumped down from her throne, put one hand on her hip, and pointed at the captives.

"Untie them!" she commanded, glaring at the chimpanzee with the crown. "That's my brother! And my dad! And Matilda!"

From behind the throne, a small and very round pirate emerged, monkeys and parrots lined up across his shoulders. With his palms pressed together, he listened to Nugget and then turned to the chimpanzee.

"Oooh! Ooh! EEeeh!" he said to the chimp, waving his arms around as his eyes flicked between Nugget and the captives. "Aak aak! AAAh, ahhh, oooh! Eeeh!"

The chimpanzee looked at the pirate, turned to Nugget, then looked at Jim. He waved a long, hairy arm lazily in the air, accompanied by some deep mumbles, and monkeys swarmed around the captives, fumbling with the knots that held them until they were free. Nugget sat back on her throne and slurped her coconut drink.

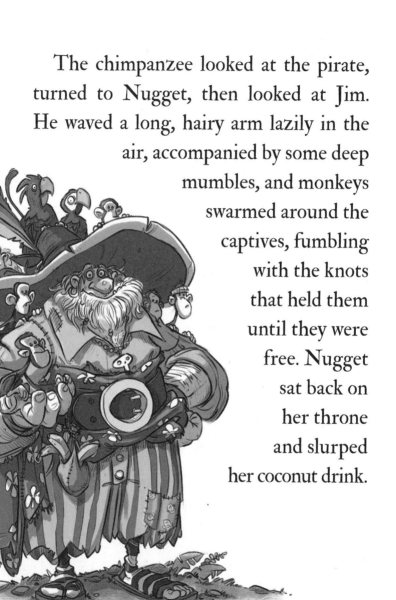

The plump pirate put his hands behind his back and stood as tall as he could, facing Jim. A couple of monkeys toppled off his shoulders as he straightened up and cleared his throat.

"His Royal Highness, King Hairy Toes, would like to welcome the family of Princess Nugget to Banana Island! He would like to apologize for any discomfort, but we have to be careful. My name is Banana Bill. Would you like a banana?"

"We're fine, thank ye kindly," said Jim. "We'd just like to take . . . um . . . Princess Nugget . . . back to our ship."

"Actually, I'd quite like another banana," said Jim's dad.

Banana Bill whispered in King Hairy Toes's ear. King Hairy Toes grumbled something back to him. Bill shuffled over to Nugget and whispered something in her ear. Nugget muttered a reply.

"Princess Nugget would like to stay a bit longer," said Bill.

"We're in a bit of a rush, you see," Matilda piped up. "We've got this treasure map that I caught on my fishing line. And we've left Jim's mom on the ship with this old fiddler and he's a little strange. We're only here to find a piece of wood for Grandpa's leg."

"A scurvy tentacle tore it from him while he slept!" added Jim. "And my grandpa is wantin' it back!"

Banana Bill gasped.

"You seek the treasure of the . . . P-P-P-Pirrrate Crrruncher?" he stuttered. "The beast who stole your grandpa's leg is also the guardian of the treasure! He eats pirates who come for his treasure!"

He turned to the king and raised his arms in the air, talking loudly in monkey-speak. "Ooooh, e-e-e-e-kee! Nom-nom-nom-arr!"

All the monkeys gasped, some scurried behind trees, several fainted, and many stood stone-still with their mouths hanging open and their tongues lolling around their knees.

King Hairy Toes climbed onto the top of his throne and addressed the monkeys.

He talked more loudly and clearly than before, with the monkeys hanging on his every word. When he'd finished speaking, he plucked a small picture from his throne. A tear rolled down his cheek as he stroked the picture before passing it to Banana Bill.

"King Hairy Toes offers to entertain Princess Nugget while ye go a-searchin' for the leg of Grandpa. The journey is too perilous for one so small," said Banana Bill, passing the small portrait to Matilda. "The king offers ye all the bananas that ye

could ever eat, if ye can find this pirate! Just like me, he was eaten by the Pirate Cruncher. I escaped, but Scurvy Sid remains in the belly of the beast."

"Um. . . . That's very kind," said Matilda, looking at the tattered painting of a burly, bearded buccaneer with a young chimpanzee on his shoulders.

"King Hairy Toes also has a *lot* of gold," whispered Banana Bill. "If bananas ain't yer thing."

"Would he also 'appen to have some banana bread?" Jim's dad asked. "My tummy's grumblin'."

"Aye, I've just baked some!" said Banana Bill. "Would ye like some coffee with that? Or some warm milk?"

"Ooh, I ain't gonna pass that up!" Jim's dad grinned. "It won't do no harm stayin' a little while, eh, Jim?"

"I 'spose not, Dad," said Jim before walking a few steps away with Matilda. "Let's find out what we can 'bout this cursed Pirate Cruncher. The more we learn 'ere, the better chance we'll 'ave of gettin' Grandpa's peg leg, and a boat full o' gold, without bein' eaten!"

10.
BANANA BILL

"Would you like more?" asked Banana Bill as a monkey thrust a heavily laden plate toward Jim and Matilda.

"Um, no thanks. I think I've had enough," said Jim with a burp.

"Me too," said Matilda. "I feel kind of sick."

Jim and Matilda were sitting on Banana Bill's veranda, outside his tree house. They could see Jim's dad and Nugget beneath them, playing tag with the monkeys.

"You escaped from the Pirate Cruncher," said Matilda. "Got any advice?"

"Turn back!" said Banana Bill, wide-eyed.

"We can't be turnin' back now," Jim said, sighing. "That beast has Grandpa's leg, and Grandpa won't rest until he gets it back! How did ye escape?"

"I was lucky," said Banana Bill. "If I were you, I'd turn back and get yer grandpa a new peg leg. But if ye really need t'know, it's all about the parrots! The monster don't like parrots!"

"So how did that help you escape?" asked Jim.

"I'd been livin' in his belly," said Bill, suddenly looking less cheery. "That place is full of pirates because he swallows 'em whole. Most 'ave been there for years, y'know, deep down in the dark, with the stomach acid bubblin' away beside 'em. I'd been there for one hundred days 'n' nights, and I had my trusty parrot, Gertrude, with me. She were the only parrot, though.

The rest of them swashbucklers had lost their birds. For some reason the Cruncher never ate the parrots, at least not if he could help it. I were hidin' Gertrude under this hat when he ate me, keepin' her safe from harm, or so I thought."

"Never ate the parrots . . . ?" muttered Matilda.

"So one mornin', Gertrude weren't there when I woke. Her perch were empty, so I went lookin' for her. I could hear her squawkin', and up in his mouth she were. So I climbed up, clingin' to bits of driftwood that were stuck in his throat, wadin' through dribble and seaweed. She were flyin' about, hollerin' and squawkin', and all in a flap. And then it 'appened. The Cruncher did this almighty sneeze." Banana Bill stroked Gertrude and gave a teary smile.

"Allergic to scarlet macaws!" said Matilda. "Of course!"

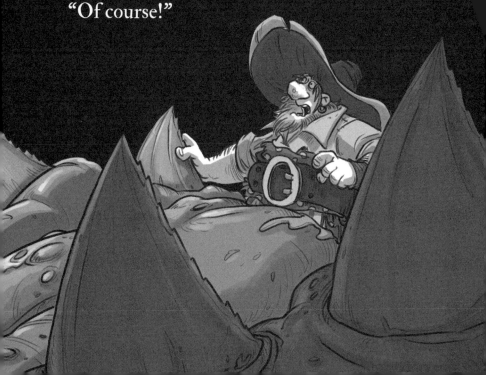

"Aye, 'tis true, Matilda!" Bill continued. "When he sneezed, we were thrown in the sea, along with everythin' else that were in his gob. Lucky for me, there were a chunk of deck that landed with a splash beside us. I ain't never been a swimmer, so I grabbed 'old of it. Me 'n' Gertrude drifted for days until we were washed up 'ere. And I've been livin' with them monkeys ever since. It ain't a bad life, is it, Gertrude?"

"So we need parrots! A *lot* of parrots!" said Matilda, with a huge smile. "This island is full of them!"

"Arrr, that'll be 'cause all of those parrots did lose their pirates when they were gobbled up by the Cruncher!" boomed Bill.

"Why do we need parrots?" asked Jim.

"Don't you remember? The fiddler told us that the Pirate Cruncher is allergic to macaws!" Matilda was inspired, talking quickly. "We're going to let the Pirate Cruncher eat us!"

"We're gonna WHAT?"

"We'll take as many parrots as we can, and keep them hidden," Matilda continued. "We can find Grandpa's leg, load up with gold,

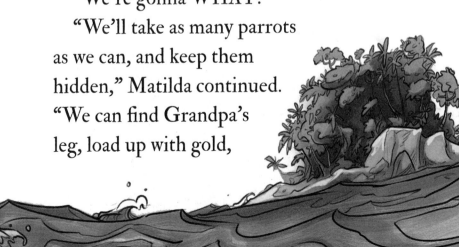

gather any pirates who are still living in its belly, and then release the parrots. When the Cruncher sneezes, we'll all be free!"

"Well! Rip me jib, it's a plan!" said Banana Bill. "I can get ye parrots! They'll come to me when I call. We just won't tell 'em what yer up to, will we, Gertrude?"

"Then we'll need to make sure we escape," said Matilda quietly.

"One more thing." Bill looked very serious. "Watch that fiddler. He ain't all he seems."

A few hours later, Jim and Matilda were on the beach with a hastily constructed wooden cage chock-full of parrots. Jim's dad had lashed the cage to the back of the car-boat. Banana Bill and Gertrude were talking to the parrots, who seemed quite relaxed sitting upon several long perches. Nugget also looked relaxed, lounging on the sand, fanned by two monkeys with long palm fronds.

"So, say yer good-byes to Matilda," said Jim's dad.

"Ain't Tilly comin' with us?"

"I don't think Matilda's folks would be too 'appy if we planned to have 'er eaten by a monster!" Jim's dad replied. "Matilda can stay 'ere, nice 'n' safe, and keep an eye on Nugget."

"But DAAAAD!" groaned Jim.

"It's OK, Jim." Matilda put a hand on his shoulder. "I've got a little something I might cobble together with Nugget. A backup, just to make sure the escape goes according to plan."

Jim trudged across the beach, following his dad, and climbed into the car-boat.

Matilda waved as they bobbed through the water, back to their ship, with the cage full of parrots squawking behind them.

"May the parrots protect ye!" Banana Bill called after them, worry etched on his brow.

11.
TREASURE!

Jim and his dad were back aboard the *Blackhole*. They'd tied the car-boat alongside the ship and left Bones sitting on the backseat, guarding the parrots.

Jim had just outlined the plan to his mom and Grandpa, and had made sure the fiddler, who was hopping around on the poop deck singing shanties, hadn't heard any of it. As Jim talked, Grandpa had been busy whittling a lump of timber he'd picked from their basket, fashioning himself a temporary leg.

"So, do ye want to join us, Grandpa?" said Jim's dad. "Me, ye, and Jim can get back yer leg from the Pirate Cruncher, we'll grab a shipful o' gold and maybe rescue a few o' them pirates!"

"Let's go!" said Grandpa, strapping his temporary peg to his leg before flinging his belt over his shoulder. "I've got an argument to finish with that beast, I 'ave."

"Grandpa can go if he wants, but you're not goin' anywhere!" said Jim's mom, glaring at her husband. "That cursed fiddler is your friend, ye invited him, so ye can stay 'ere! I've had enough of his singin' for one day!"

"But I want to . . ." mumbled Jim's dad.

She gave him a kiss on the cheek, grabbed the keys to the vehicle from out of his hands, and climbed down the rope ladder and into the driver's seat.

The old fiddler appeared over the *Blackhole*'s rail and serenaded them with a shanty as they chugged away.

"Off you go, boys, but I think
I'll stay here!
I doubt what you find will
bring you good cheer.
For a pile of old metal you
don't really need
has brought on a dangerous
case of greed!

And being greedy, you know,
is wrong,
which brings me at last to the
end of my so —"

"Oh, be quiet!" grumbled Jim's dad.

The *chug-chug-chug* of the car-boat had sent Grandpa to sleep. Squawk was snoring on his shoulder, and Bones was fast asleep across his lap. Jim was sitting cross-legged on the front of the vehicle, scanning the horizon with a telescope.

"LAND AHOY!" he yelled, pointing to a solitary palm tree in the distance.

Jim's mom turned to port a little and opened the throttle. Jim climbed around the windshield and toward the rear of the boat, where the cage of parrots was perched.

"Shhhh!" said Jim, with his finger to his lips. "Ye'll need to be quiet now. Just fer a while!"

Jim pulled a tarpaulin up around the cage and shackled the top closed with a lock and chain. He hung the key around his neck and jumped into the front seat, next to his mom.

"Do ye think it'll wait for us to climb ashore, Mom? Before it eats us?"

"I reckon it will," said his mom. "I'll drive on yonder sand and we'll see what happens. Maybe fasten yer seatbelt and stay in the vehicle. We'll be tossed about like a force ten before we end up in its tummy."

As they drew nearer to the island, Jim spotted an enormous treasure chest beneath the palm tree, overflowing with gold coins, trinkets, and precious stones. He thought he saw the island move a little, but maybe that was just the bobbing of the car-boat. As they hit land, Jim's mom disengaged the propeller and the vehicle's wheels spun in the sand, lurching alongside the booty. Grandpa woke up with a loud snort.

"ARRR! Curses! Where's that scurvy beast? Let me at 'im!" he yelled and clambered over the side of the car-boat, hobbling across the sand with his cutlass held high. Bones ran around and around in circles, barking, and Squawk fluttered into the palm tree and screeched "TENTACLE!" at the top of his voice.

"That's the first time
Grandpa's been ashore since
1949," Jim's mom said with a sigh.

Grandpa turned to look at them.
"Where is it? Where is the b —?"

Grandpa's face, and cutlass, dropped.
He was staring beyond Jim and up into
the air. Jim and his mom looked over

their shoulders to see two gargantuan eyes looking down at them. The island shifted, and Jim felt the car-boat rise beneath him. As he grabbed hold of his seat, huge pointed teeth filled his vision, and then . . .

12.
THE BELLY OF THE BEAST

They ended up at the back of the Pirate Cruncher's mouth. Amazingly, the vehicle was upright, floating in a pool of saliva. Grandpa and Bones were standing on the tongue and peering down the monster's throat, into the darkness. There was no sign of Squawk.

"I ain't sure this is such a good idea," said Grandpa. "Yer made yer plan on the word of the squab who lives with the monkeys, y'say?"

"Maybe ye'd best hop aboard, Grandpa," said Jim.

He whistled, and Bones bounded across the fleshy

surface and jumped onto Jim's knee. There were murmurings from the parrots, who were still covered by the tarpaulin. Jim's mom turned the key, and the vehicle's engine spluttered to life. Grandpa climbed into the back and buckled his seatbelt.

But before they could drive anywhere, there was a mighty gurgling and a wave of liquid gushed from the monster's gut, splashing against the sides of the car-boat. The tongue lifted, and the vehicle surged upward and was thrown into the darkness.

Jim's mom was steering, but had very little control as they surfed the wave of saliva down toward the Pirate Cruncher's belly. At times the wheels would make contact with the walls of the throat and they'd speed along, before being lifted again by the stream of juices. They landed with a splash in a great bubbling puddle littered with bones and jetsam.

In the gloom, Jim could make out ramshackle buildings constructed from sections of ships, tattered sails, and upturned boats. Candles and oil lamps flickered, illuminating

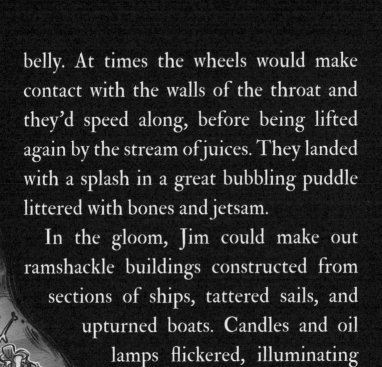

the dark, damp confines of the beast's enormous stomach. Jim's mom put the vehicle into gear and switched on the headlights, and they trundled slowly toward the shacks. Bones hopped onto the front of the vehicle, sniffing the briny air.

The candlelight threw large shadows of figures scurrying around amid the shacks onto the stomach walls, but Jim couldn't see anyone. The makeshift town was eerily quiet. A dark, tattered shape dashed across their path. Bones growled. A head popped up from behind an upturned rowboat, and the vehicle came to a halt.

"WHO ARE YE?" screeched a voice.

"We are the Jolley-Rogers!" Jim shouted, peering into the darkness.

There were murmurings and the sound of movement. More shadowy shapes popped up here and there, in hats and rags, with wild hair and long beards, all peering at Jim with glaring eyes. Some held lanterns aloft, which only made their faces look creepier as the flickering light cast hard shadows across their grizzled features.

"WHAT DO YOU WANT?"
hollered a croaky voice.

"TREASURE, NO DOUBT!" yelled
another, followed by cackles of laughter.

"We are here to help ye all ESCAPE!"
Jim replied.

The Cruncher's stomach filled
with the sound of delirious laughter.
More pirates popped up between
the timbers and canvas and broken

boats, holding their sides, pointing at the Jolley-Rogers, and guffawing.

"THERE AIN'T NO ESCAPE!" They laughed.

"WE HAVE A PLAN!" Jim shouted from the back of the car-boat, where he was unshackling the tarpaulin. "AND WE BROUGHT PARROTS!"

As the tarpaulin fell from the sides of the cage, there was silence. The pirates were motionless, staring teary-eyed at the parrots.

"WHO'S A PRETTY BOY?" squawked a parrot.

13.
THE VOTE

"You see," said Jim's mom, "the Pirate Cruncher's allergic to macaws, and these 'ere parrots can help ye all escape."

The pirates were barely listening. They had surrounded the cage and were cooing over their long-lost parrots. Some tickled their parrots' heads through the bars. All of the pirates looked very happy.

"Do ye remember Banana Bill?" asked Jim.

"Aye!" said a wrinkled pirate captain with a threadbare hat and a beard that almost reached the ground. "He were my first mate, so he was. But he disappeared one day. Went lookin' for his parrot, never to return. Fell in them scurvy stomach juices, no doubt, and slipped into the Cruncher's bowels. Shame, he were a lovely chap."

"No!" said Jim. "He's alive! He's livin' on an island not far from 'ere, with a thousand parrots!"

"And quite a lot of monkeys," added Grandpa.

Jim retold the story of Banana Bill's escape. As he spoke, the old pirates pulled up crates and barrels to sit on, cracked open bottles of grog, and stroked their beards. Then Jim told them Matilda's escape plan. By the time he had finished, every pirate in the Pirate Cruncher's belly was rapt, apart from Grandpa, who had drunk quite a lot of grog and was once again snoring in the back of the car-boat.

"We need to vote!" hollered a huge purple-bearded pirate who looked as old as the sea. His hair had gone gray, but a purple hue somehow remained in his beard. "We vote on everythin' down 'ere, don't we, lads? So, who's in favor of the plan?"

Almost all of the arms shot in the air, along with a few hooks.

Only one pirate voted against the plan. He was Alfred of 'Averford West, a pale, bedraggled rogue with a nervous tic and clothes that seemed to wriggle as he walked.

"I've never been too keen on the sea," he mumbled nervously. "All that sky and ocean and wide, open beaches. I like it down 'ere in the dark, with my friends." He stroked a rat sitting on his knee, which then disappeared beneath his doublet.

"So!" said Purplebeard. "Only one against! We will follow the plan!"

The pirates cheered, swinging their bottles of grog in the air and dancing around.

"We need to build some rafts," shouted Jim's mom above the merriment. "Cobble together some of this timber and lash it good and strong. Fix up some sails and maybe some oars. How many pirates are ye?"

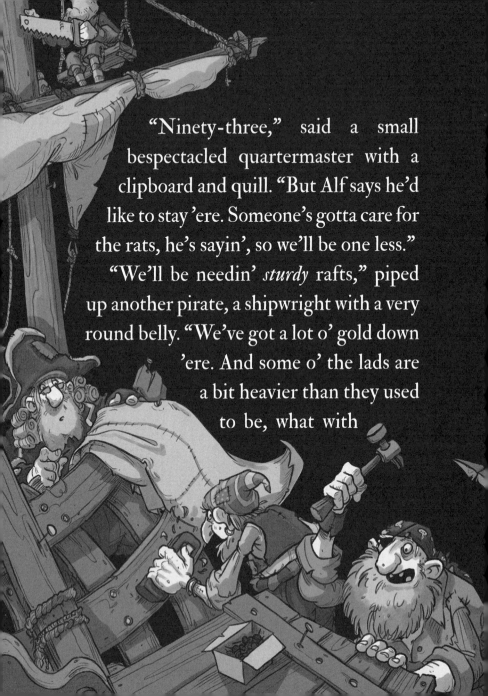

"Ninety-three," said a small bespectacled quartermaster with a clipboard and quill. "But Alf says he'd like to stay 'ere. Someone's gotta care for the rats, he's sayin', so we'll be one less."

"We'll be needin' *sturdy* rafts," piped up another pirate, a shipwright with a very round belly. "We've got a lot o' gold down 'ere. And some o' the lads are a bit heavier than they used to be, what with all the fish and hardtack and molasses and chocolate, and all thar' sittin' about. It ain't good for your waistline."

The pirates set about building the rafts. For a bunch of gnarly old-timers with an average age of eighty-something, they were remarkably energetic and had forgotten little of their knot-tying and ship-fixing skills. They sang while they worked, accompanied by the tunes of a skeletal accordion player and some of the parrots, who squawked and shrieked and sang along.

When they were done, Jim's mom checked her watch.

"It'll be sunset within the hour," she said. "We should get movin' onto the Cruncher's tongue and make our escape before dark. All aboard, me hearties!"

The pirates had built three large rafts, tethered to one another in a line, with the foremost raft chained to the car-boat's towing eye. The rafts were laden with chests and barrels, full to the brim with treasure. Each had a mast and a sail, and oars shackled to the sides, should the wind be blowing the wrong way. The pirates clambered aboard their creations, in a hubbub of excitement and expectation.

"Are we all aboard?" shouted Jim's mom from the driver's seat. She looked past the parrot cage to see the three rafts, packed full of pirates who were all nodding vigorously.

"Wait! Where's Bones?" said Jim. "We can't leave 'til we 'ave Bones aboard!"

Jim hopped down from the vehicle and ran among the deserted shacks, whistling and calling. He was beginning to worry when Bones appeared from the gloom, bounding across the debris on the stomach floor with something wooden in his mouth.

"Grandpa's peg leg! Good boy!" Jim rubbed Bones's head and ran back to the car-boat. Bones jumped onto the backseat next to Grandpa, wagging his tail with the peg leg firmly clenched between his teeth. Grandpa snorted a little but didn't wake up.

The vehicle rumbled to life, the ropes and chains pulled taut, and the train of pirates and gold skidded through the bubbling juices and up the Pirate Cruncher's throat.

11.
Aaa-Choooo!

The vehicle was moving up the Pirate Cruncher's tongue. Jim's mom was checking the ropes and chains to be sure they would all hold together when they landed in the sea. Jim thought he could hear the monster sniffling, even with the parrots secured in the cage. He was waiting on the back of the car-boat, ready to set them free. When his mom climbed in and gave the all clear, he turned the key in the padlock.

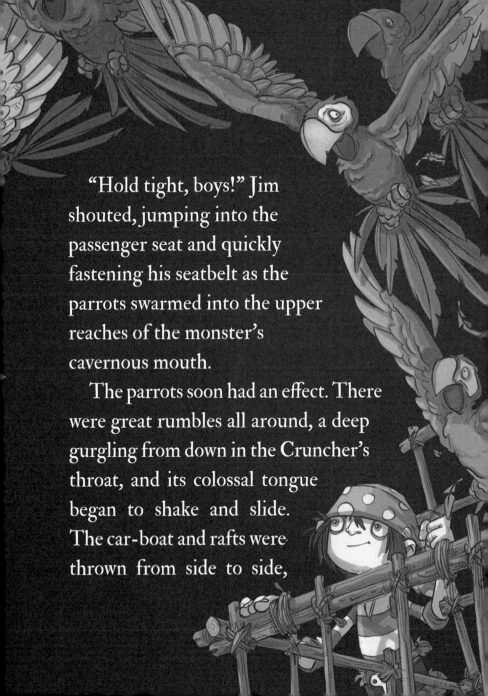

"Hold tight, boys!" Jim shouted, jumping into the passenger seat and quickly fastening his seatbelt as the parrots swarmed into the upper reaches of the monster's cavernous mouth.

The parrots soon had an effect. There were great rumbles all around, a deep gurgling from down in the Cruncher's throat, and its colossal tongue began to shake and slide. The car-boat and rafts were thrown from side to side, and everyone held on tight as the parrots fluttered above their heads.

The Cruncher took a deep breath, and a gust of warm air hit them like a hurricane, hurling seaweed, bones, and debris all around. Before it caught its breath, the beast inhaled again. Sitting in the front of the vehicle felt like riding a roller coaster, thought Jim, as the tongue puckered up into the roof of the Cruncher's mouth.

He grabbed hold of the dashboard as another gust of sea air blasted past them. He heard the shouts of the old pirates, who were clinging to their rafts as they swung above the Cruncher's gaping throat.

And then . . .

AAAA ...
AAAAAAA ...
AAA-CHOOOOOO!

They flew through the air, landing in the sea with an almighty splash, the rafts strung out behind it. Some pirates lost their grip and fell into the sea but were thrown life belts by their mates and dragged alongside as Jim's mom floored the vehicle's accelerator. One rickety pirate was standing on a plank of wood, gripping a length of rope and screaming as he surfed along behind the rearmost raft.

Fortunately for him, the Pirate Cruncher was still dazed and sniffling, rubbing its nostrils with a tattered sail gripped in its tentacle.

With a happy flap of his wings, Squawk appeared from nowhere and perched himself on Grandpa's hat.

"Eh? What!?" said Grandpa, suddenly waking and sitting bolt upright on the backseat. "Five gobstoppers and a packet of . . . Oh. Um. Where's the cursed beast? Where's it gone? Where's me leg?"

"The beast is behind ye, Grandpa!" Jim answered. "And yer leg's on the seat."

Grandpa pulled out his telescope and looked over the stern. The Pirate Cruncher had recovered. It raised itself from the sea, teeth glinting in the sun and tentacles swirling in the air all around. Its eyes narrowed, and a wave formed across its stomach as it hurtled their way.

The pirates had spotted the Pirate Cruncher too and began firing the cannons at it. Most of the shots sploshed into the sea, but the cannonballs that hit the beast bounced harmlessly off its thick, barnacle-encrusted skin.

"TENTACLE!" shrieked Squawk.

The waves parted as an immense tentacle thrust upward, high into the air. It snaked its way toward the Jolley-Rogers and began encircling the car-boat. Grandpa swung his cutlass at the suckers and shouted seafaring insults. A swarm of parrots flew around the tentacle, and it dropped beneath the water, resurfacing on the starboard side.

"LAND AHOY!" yelled Jim, spotting Banana Island through the windshield wipers. "Nearly there!"

It was only the parrots that were keeping the Pirate Cruncher at bay. It swatted at them as they

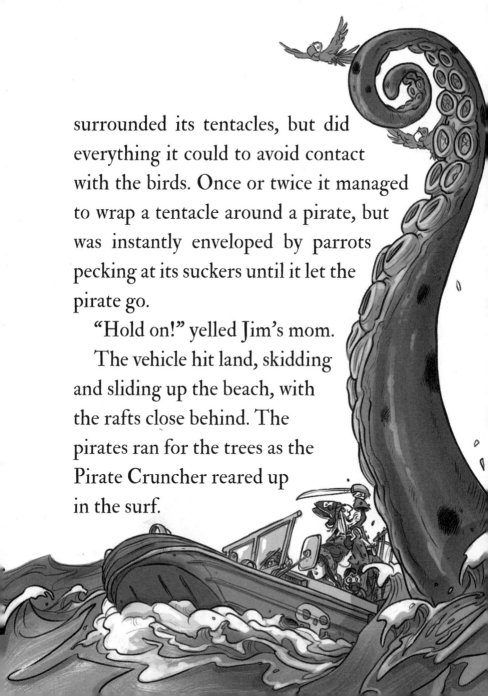

surrounded its tentacles, but did
everything it could to avoid contact
with the birds. Once or twice it managed
to wrap a tentacle around a pirate, but
was instantly enveloped by parrots
pecking at its suckers until it let the
pirate go.

"Hold on!" yelled Jim's mom.

The vehicle hit land, skidding
and sliding up the beach, with
the rafts close behind. The
pirates ran for the trees as the
Pirate Cruncher reared up
in the surf.

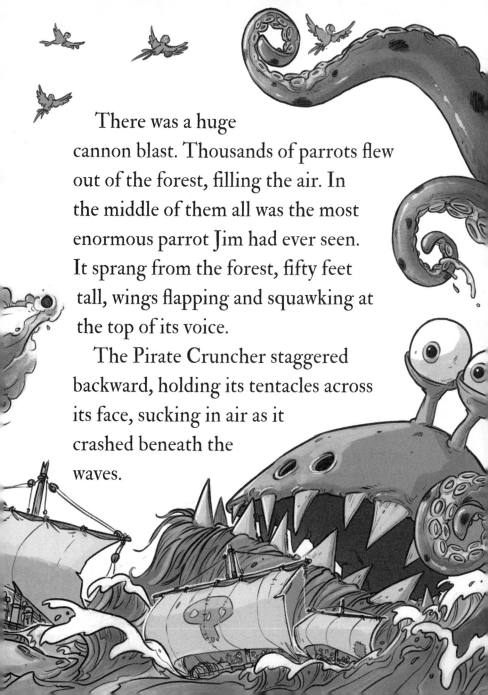

There was a huge cannon blast. Thousands of parrots flew out of the forest, filling the air. In the middle of them all was the most enormous parrot Jim had ever seen. It sprang from the forest, fifty feet tall, wings flapping and squawking at the top of its voice.

The Pirate Cruncher staggered backward, holding its tentacles across its face, sucking in air as it crashed beneath the waves.

15.
FAREWELLS

"Hiya, Jim!" said Matilda, poking her head out of the enormous parrot's mouth. Her voice was amplified by a megaphone.

Nugget appeared next to her, with a monkey on her head. "Do you like what we made?"

"It's perfect!" Jim replied. "That'll keep the Pirate Cruncher away for good!"

The bedraggled pirates gathered on the beach. Parrots fluttered in from the trees and landed on their shoulders. Monkeys

scampered
from the forest,
climbing up the
trees and covering the
rocks along the shore. King Hairy
Toes arrived on a portable throne carried
by four burly monkeys, accompanied
by a drumroll and Banana Bill,
who offered everyone a reward.

The pirates came forward, one by one, to be presented with a banana. A stout pirate with a bald head and an octopus tattoo stumbled to the front of the line, struggling to see through his homemade spectacles.

"Aaah-ooh! Eeeh! Seeed! Seeeed!" squealed King Hairy Toes, springing from his throne. He flew across the sand, through the air, and engulfed the stout pirate in a hug, peppering his cheeks with slobbery kisses.

"Oh my, it's Sturdy Sid!" said Banana Bill, translating. "Kiss, kiss, kiss."

"Hairy Toes! Is that you?" said Sturdy Sid, crying with joy. "I thought the beast had eaten ye! For years, I thought ye to be gobbled up! I thought about ye every day! And here ye are . . . a king!"

King Hairy Toes pulled a ragged teddy bear from his throne along with the portrait he had shown Jim and Matilda.

He passed the bear to Sturdy Sid and held the portrait alongside Sid's face, flicking his eyes back and forth.

"Um, this is prob'ly a good time to be leavin'," said Jim's mom. "'Twas lovely to meet ye all, but we be needin' to get Matilda back to Dull-on-Sea before her parents start to worry. I'll thank ye on behalf of my husband for all the banana bread he ate. And thank ye for lookin' after Nugget. She's had a lovely time."

"Sid, will ye be stayin' with King Hairy Toes?" asked Jim Lad. "Or comin' with us?"

"I've found me best mate!" gushed Sturdy Sid. "And I like a banana, so I'll stay 'ere!"

"Ah! Ah! Ooooooh!" said King Hairy Toes, opening a huge chest of gold. "Aka! Aka! Nananana, eeeh!"

"Take some extra gold!" Banana Bill translated. "And we've loaded the rafts with ample bananas for your journey!"

The old pirates cheered and clambered back onto their rafts. Nugget gave King Hairy Toes a big hug and climbed into the car-boat, between Grandpa and Matilda. Jim toppled the cage off the stern of the vehicle, and a horde of monkeys hoisted the treasure chest in its place.

The Jolley-Rogers and the pirates waved good-bye to King Hairy Toes, the monkeys, Sturdy Sid, and Banana Bill, and the car-boat burbled into the sea, tugging the rafts behind it. They pulled alongside the *Blackhole*, and Jim scurried onto the deck to secure the ropes.

"Evenin', Jim!" came a voice from the fo'c'sle. "Look at this! I finally got around to tarrin' them deadeyes. Amazin' what ye can get done with a bit o' peace and quiet!"

"Where's the fiddler?" Jim asked.

"Arr, he disappeared not long after you left," Jim's dad replied. "He said somethin' about lunch before skippin'

off the end of the bowsprit and flyin' through the air into the distance, which were peculiar 'cause he never ate no grub."

"What are we goin' to do with all these pesky pirates?" said Grandpa, strapping on his trusty old peg leg. "There ain't room for 'em on the *Blackhole*."

"Don't ye worry. I know just the place," said Jim's mom.

16.
FOGGY HEAD

The *Blackhole* sailed into Dullshire Sound just after dawn, cutting through a light sea mist with the sun as it streamed across the waves. Jim and Matilda were watching the sunrise from the poop deck. Below them, Grandpa scanned the horizon while Jim's mom steered the ship.

Up ahead, a small boat was coming out of Dull-on-Sea harbor and heading their way. A uniformed man on deck was scrutinizing the

Blackhole through a pair of binoculars. Jim and Matilda waved from the poop deck, but he didn't wave back.

"Hello! Dull-on-Sea customs to the pirate ship! Anything to declare? Over," came a voice on the radio.

"Um. . . . Only ninety-one retired pirates," Jim's dad replied into his handset. "And an equal number of parrots. Oh, and a lot of bananas."

"I'm sorry, the line's a bit fuzzy. I thought you said 'retired pirates,'" the voice replied with a chuckle. "Over."

"Um, yes. That's what I said. But don't ye worry, they're mostly good citizens and they've got barrels full o' gold!"

"I think we may have to come aboard. Please hold your position!" said the voice.

"Tell 'em we're headin' to Foggy Head," said Jim's mom.

"Hello, Cap'n Customs! We're bound for Foggy Head Retirement Home, and these old sea dogs are all booked in. Ye can chat to the matron if ye like." Jim's dad crossed his fingers — things never went well when the customs men came aboard. They weren't too keen on skulls and treasure and cannons and stuff.

"Carry on to Foggy Head. . . . Um, over," came a slightly confused voice from the customs boat.

The sitting room at Foggy Head Retirement Home was full to the brim. Ninety-three old pirates sat on leather armchairs, snacking and watching a puppet show, with their parrots dozing on their shoulders.

"The puppet-show man always comes on a Tuesday," said the matron. "I've been turning him away of late, as we only had two residents. There aren't too many old pirates nowadays, and the puppets always got Blood-Blister Bob a bit excited. Before you'd know it, he'd have his cutlass out, which would then set off Grumpy Gordon. Hopefully they'll calm down a bit with a few more friends. We have crochet club on Wednesdays, dancing on Thursdays, and exercise on Friday afternoons, before they get their rum."

Jim's mom smiled and shook the matron's hand. "I'm sure they'll all be very happy here."

"You know, we were on the verge of closing," the matron continued. "But now we'll be open for years and years with all that lovely gold! Thank you so much!"

The matron walked them to the front door and hurried back to her new residents.

Outside, Matilda and the Jolley-Rogers walked past the Foggy Head caretaker, who huffed and puffed as he shoveled treasure into a wheelbarrow and poured it down the coal chute at the side of the building.

They strolled through the gardens toward the jetty where the *Blackhole* was moored, happy that the old pirates had a new home with daylight and parrots, and no bubbling stomach acid around their feet. The Jolley-Rogers had put aside a little bit of treasure for themselves, and Grandpa was busy counting coins on deck.

"Hey, Grandpa, it won't be long 'til ye'll be comin' 'ere!" said Jim Lad, giggling as they climbed aboard the ship.

Grandpa grimaced, leaned back in his rocking chair, and threw his blanket over his knees. "Bah! I got life in me yet, boy!"

"Righto, let's get Matilda home!" said Jim's dad, rolling out a chart.

"Aye, aye, Cap'n!" said Nugget, hopping on her barrel at the helm.

"TENTACLE!" squawked Squawk.

Don't miss Jim Lad and Matilda's
other swashbuckling adventures!

In stores now!